Kane and the Christmas Football Adventure

AD.   ⅃BLEY

For Sebastian

Books by Adrian Lobley

Learning Maths
The Football Maths Book (Ages 4-7)
The Football Maths Book - The Re-match! (Ages 5-8)
The Football Maths Book - The Christmas Match (Ages 6-8)
The Football Maths Book - The Birthday Party (Ages 7-8)
The Football Maths Book - The World Cup (Age 9-10)

Learning to Read
A Learn to Read Book: The Football Match (Ages 4-5)
A Learn to Read Book: The Tennis Match (Ages 4-5)

Historical Fiction
Kane and the Mystery of the Missing World Cup (Ages 7-10)
Kane and the Christmas Football Adventure (Ages 7-10)

Humour
The Ridiculous Adventures of Sidebottom and McPlop (Ages 7-10)

For more info go to: www.adrianlobley.com

First published in 2018

ISBN-13: 978-1986839327
ISBN-10: 198683932X

ACKNOWLEDGMENTS

With thanks to Mum, Dad, Sebastian, Sarah, Kaden, Callan, Asher, Logan and Derry for reviewing and providing feedback on the book.

Cover designed by Alyssa Josue

Chapter 1

Kane the dog pushed open the door of his master's bedroom with his nose. He could see Adam asleep in bed. Kane had just been looking out of the window in the lounge and had seen a most extraordinary sight. He was so excited he jumped up onto the bed on top of Adam and started licking his face. Adam woke with a start.

"Kane, stop licking my face. What is it boy?" Kane jumped down to the floor and bounded over to Adam's window and barked at the curtains which were closed.

"What is it? What's outside?" Adam looked at his clock, which read, '9:30am, 17th December.' "Brilliant," Adam exclaimed, "only 8 days until Christmas Day!" He threw his duvet off and climbed out of bed. Walking over to the curtains he pulled them back, not quite sure of what he was about to see.

As the curtains drew back, instead of the usual green gardens outside his bedroom window, he was greeted by the most amazing scene. The whole village was covered in six inches of white snow. Other than the postman's footprints the sheet of white had been totally undisturbed. Kane barked with excitement.

"Wow, look at all that snow!"

Adam grabbed his clothes from the wardrobe and started putting them on. "Come on, let's have breakfast and then go and play. We can try football in the snow." Adam looked at the posters of his favourite Premier League team, Newcastle United, which covered his walls. He grinned.

The house was covered in Christmas decorations and as Adam ducked under the paper chains he had made with his mum, which stretched from one side of the landing ceiling to the other, he breathed in the familiar smell of toast and bacon wafting up from the kitchen. "Cool! Bacon sandwiches!" He ran down the stairs, with Kane in hot pursuit, and skidded into the kitchen. His mum and dad were already eating.

"Adam, your bacon and toast are in the oven, keeping warm."

"Thanks mum." Adam brought his bacon sandwich through and sat at the table.

"Wow, what's the rush?" His dad asked him as he watched Adam wolfing his food down. "Ah, don't tell me," his dad smiled, "the snow?" Adam nodded enthusiastically.

"Hey dad, who are top of the Premier League, after the matches last night?"

"Don't worry, Newcastle won 4-1 and are still top." His dad said, as he turned over the page in his newspaper.

"Yesss, get in!" Adam pumped his fist.

"I've put your Wellington boots near the fire to warm them up," said Adam's mum, "I knew you'd want to go out."

"Great, thanks." After eating his bacon sandwich Adam sat in front of their crackling log fire and pulled on his Wellies.

"Assuming you're going to be playing out with your friends most of today, I've made you a pack lunch and there's something in there for Kane too." His mum handed him a little bag of supplies.

"Thanks, mum." Adam took them, grabbed his rucksack and stuffed them inside. He checked his football was in it too and then slotted his favourite football book in as well. Pulling on his gloves and coat, he slung the rucksack over his shoulder and opened the front door.

"Come on boy, let's go to the big park near Buckingham Palace." Kane raced out of the house and Adam followed, his boots making a 'crump' sound as he stepped into the deep snow.

The snow had started falling again and the pair ran past some younger children who were giggling with delight as they threw snowballs at each other.

"This is great Kane, it's the school holidays, plus we've got snow as well!"

For the next hour in the park Adam built his own little igloo, with Kane leaping about barking with excitement.

"I don't know how to build a roof on my igloo, Kane. It keeps falling in," sighed Adam after the third failed attempt, "but at least I've made walls and an entrance." Adam packed the last clump of snow onto the wall. "There, it's officially finished." He stepped back to proudly examine his work.

"I'm shattered. Let's sit inside and I'll read some of my football book to you." Kane wagged his tail and entered the igloo. It was very cosy. Nobody outside could see either of them.

"You'll never believe how football used to be played in the olden days, Kane," Adam sat on the snow floor and opened his book, "it says here that the first official football match was in 1863. Wow, that's ages ago! It took place here in England but there were no rules set about how long a match should last or how many people were on each team!" Kane cocked his head to the side, showing his surprise. Kane was a particularly clever dog and had been trained to understand a lot of what people say.

"Hey, there were no crossbars back then, just posts! How cool is that, you could just score every time. You just boot it really high." Adam laughed. "Wouldn't it be brilliant if we could get to see the first ever football match!"

He read some more, "Plus the first ever match was 15 a-side! No wonder it ended 0-0 then. As soon as one of the players got the ball, they'd just be tackled." Adam turned the page as he sat happily in his own little snow home.

"The first ever match was Barnes versus Richmond." He paused. "I've never heard of either of them as football clubs." Adam thought some more. "I've heard of the places called Barnes and also Richmond, they're at the other side of London." He frowned as he read on. "Ah, here it says that Richmond focused on Rugby, not football and Barnes played football for a number of years but ended up concentrating on Rugby too. That explains why I've not seen their names in the Premier League."

Adam could feel his trousers getting damp as he sat on the packed snow inside the igloo. "I'm hungry, Kane. Let's find somewhere to sit and we can have our food."

The pair found a bench at the edge of the field and Adam gave Kane the dog treats his mum had packed and then tucked into his sandwiches and crisps.

In front of them a couple of families were building snow barricades and then started making snowballs and stockpiling them behind their barricades.

"These guys are spending a lot of time preparing for their snowball fight, Kane," said an impressed Adam. "I wonder if they'll let us join in if I offer to make some snowballs too." Kane woofed. "I think I might go and ask them."

Before long Adam was on his knees crouched behind one of the barriers, with one of the families, launching snowballs at the other family. Kane was having a great time running around trying to catch the snowballs in his mouth, although without much success.

One or two other children, that Adam knew from the neighbourhood, came over and asked if they could join in. The families welcomed them and the snowball fight went on for another two hours.

Eventually everyone was exhausted and the two families announced that they were going home. Adam thanked them for letting him play. The other children headed off too.

"Come on, Kane, let's go for a

game of football. We'll head over to that sheltered area where the trees are. There's some grass there, so you can dribble the ball with your nose much easier than in the snow."

Adam and Kane ran as fast as they could towards the other side of the park. "Hey Kane, look!" Adam pointed as they approached the goal. "There's no crossbar on that goal, just two posts." Adam stopped running and walked towards the posts. He laughed. "Just like the first official football match between Barnes and Richmond in 1863!" Adam frowned. "I could have sworn there was a crossbar when I looked over earlier though." He shrugged. "Oh well, I must have been mistaken."

Adam hadn't been mistaken though.

Something strange was happening.

And little did Adam know, any second now, he and his magical dog were going to embark on one of the most exciting adventures of their lives.

Chapter 2

Adam stood between the two goal posts which were in front of a hedge and trees, the branches of which hung over the area in front of him. He kicked his football and Kane chased after it. It landed in the snow but Kane managed to nuzzle the ball back onto the grassy area and then dribbled it with his nose back in Adam's direction. As Kane weaved his way towards Adam he suddenly left the ball where it was and ran towards his master.

"Kane, what are you doing? You've left the ball behind." Kane began barking as he approached Adam, who held out his arms for Kane to jump into, for a hug.

But Kane didn't jump.

In fact, he ran straight past Adam and between the posts behind him.

Adam, a bit surprised, turned round.

But he couldn't see Kane.

His dog had completely disappeared!

Something incredible had happened.

"Huh? Where's he gone?" Adam looked all around but Kane wasn't anywhere to be seen. "He must have run through the thick hedge somehow," thought Adam.

Just then, Adam looked down on the ground at what looked like a thick line of snow stretching from one goal post to the other goal post, on top of the grass. All of a sudden the line of snow started to fade. "What on earth...?"

Adam realised it wasn't snow.

It was a painted line.

One that hadn't been there when they had arrived.

It was vanishing very quickly.

"Kane?" Adam stuttered, as he realised what had just happened. Kane hadn't gone through the hedge. He had vanished when he crossed the white line.

Adam had seen this happen before.

A few months ago Kane and Adam had travelled back through time to the year 1966 by stepping over a white painted line in a mysterious goal they had come across. They only had the time that the painted white line stayed in place, to cross over it and travel in time though.

Once the line had vanished, it just returned to being a normal goal.

Adam suddenly came to his senses. He realised that Kane was no longer here and that when his canine friend had crossed over the white painted line, he had travelled through to a different time period.

Adam knew he had to either jump over the line right now and follow Kane and travel through time too, or stay in the present and possibly lose his dog forever! The line had now almost vanished.

"Kane!" Adam shouted.

He didn't have time to grab his football. Adam just scooped up his backpack and leapt forward into the goal.

But had he left it too late?

Had the line already vanished, leaving Adam in the present and

Kane stranded forever in another time?

Chapter 3

Adam's feet landed on the ground and squelched in a mud puddle. The hedge and trees that were in front of him had suddenly disappeared.

"You're there!" exclaimed Adam as he saw Kane in front of him. Kane leapt into his arms.

"Thank goodness, I thought I'd lost you." He gave his beloved dog a huge hug. "The trees have gone and so has all the snow," Adam said as he looked all around, "we must have travelled through time again!" Adam's heart was racing with excitement. "Where are we though, this looks nothing like the big park we were in?"

Adam turned to look at the two goal posts they had passed through. There was no crossbar still and the white painted line vanished before his eyes.

"How did you do that?" said a young urchin boy who was walking up to them. "You and your dog appeared from nowhere!" The urchin, who was covered in dirt and grime and wore tatty old clothes, studied Adam, before continuing, "look at them clothes you're wearing too, you must be posh. 'ere, are you rich? I've never seen clothes like them before."

"You ask a lot of questions," replied Adam. "Where are your shoes?" Adam was looking down at the boy's muddy feet.

"I don't 'ave none."

"But it's December? It's freezing."

"Don't make no difference. We're too poor to 'ave shoes." Adam raised his eyebrows in surprise before gathering his thoughts. "What year is this?" he asked the urchin.

"Why, it's 1863. 'as been 1863 all year. It's 17th December. Only eight days to Christmas day!"

Even though Adam knew they had travelled back in time, it was still a shock to hear how far back they had gone. Last time they had travelled to 1966 which seemed so long in the past, but this was now over 100 years further back, in 1863!

" 'ere you wanna be careful with 'im." The boy was pointing at Kane. "Dog snatchers 'ang about this park. You've got a shiny dog. They'll make a lot of money if they steal 'im and sell 'im." Kane whined when he heard this.

"I'm sure we'll be fine." Adam replied. He needed more information about where they were.

"This park's near Buckingham Palace, right?" Adam asked.

"Bucking'am Palace? Where Queen Victoria lives? Nah, it's a long walk from there," exclaimed the urchin boy. He frowned at Adam. "So, you don't know what year it is and you don't even know where you are?"

"So where are we?" Adam said, ignoring the boy's comment.

"Barnes, of course. This is Limes Field."

Adam raised his eyebrows in further surprise at the news. He looked at Kane and whispered, "We've not just moved back in time, we've also moved places, Kane." His dog barked.

Just then the wind blew in a different direction and Adam recoiled at the smell of the boy.

"Wow, you need a bath, you stink." said Adam before he realised how rude his words had sounded.

"I 'ad me bath five days ago!" exclaimed the boy, "I don't 'ave to 'ave another one for a bit. I 'ate bath time, Ma scrubs too 'ard."

Suddenly, from behind the boys, a man started shouting at them, "You boys! Get off that football pitch!"

"It's Ebenezer Morley!" squealed the urchin, "Come on, run!" he said to Adam and Kane.

"Who's Ebenezer Morley?" shouted Adam as they ran as fast as they could off the pitch.

"He's the one organising the very first football match in two days time.

It's Barnes versus Richmond on Saturday." The boy panted as he ran.

Kane ran on ahead as he didn't like being shouted at. Eventually the boys came to a stop at the edge of Limes Field. They had got away from Ebenezer Morley.

"Seeing as I'm here in 1863, I'd love to see the match on Saturday." Adam said to his new friend.

"We could watch it together," said the boy, "my name's Joseph."

"Definitely. I'm Adam and this is Kane…" Adam looked behind him to see where Kane was.

He wasn't there.

In fact, he was nowhere to be seen.

In the distance he heard some frightened barking.

"That's Kane barking. I recognise it. He only barks like that when he's in trouble. Something's wrong!"

Adam couldn't see him. "He must be behind that thick row of trees." Adam started running in the direction of the barking. As he rounded the trees he saw, to his horror, two men bundling Kane into the back of a cart. Kane was wriggling to try and escape from the men but they were too strong.

"Kane!!" shouted Adam in horror, as he watched Kane being shoved inside a small wooden cage which was on the back of the cart.

"Go, go, go!" shouted the huge man on the back of the cart. His smaller companion grabbed the reins of the horse as the cart set off at a furious pace in the opposite direction to Adam.

"Kane! They've got Kane. Someone help!!"

But there were no adults around to

hear Adam's cries.

Adam ran as fast as he could after the cart but they had a head start and the horse that pulled the cart was too quick. Eventually the cart went round a corner and out of sight.

The dog snatchers had captured Kane.

"Kane..." Adam said helplessly. He came to a stop, completely out of breath. "They've kidnapped my dog..."

Adam's heart sank. The men had gone. His beloved canine had been kidnapped and there was nothing he could do about it.

Chapter 4

After a mile the horse and cart slowed. "It's okay," said the big man, "they couldn't keep up with us. I've put their dog in one of the cages." He looked at the four cages. "Let's get all these dogs back to the building." The smaller man nodded and used the horse's reins to steer the cart down a nearby cobbled street.

After a bumpy fifteen minute journey, they approached a large wooden building.

"Wooah there." shouted the driver to the horse, which obediently came to a stop.

"Give me a hand with these," the big man said to the driver. The pair started lifting the wooden cages, each containing a dog, into the building.

Kane looked at the other three dogs, one of which was clearly very old and unwell.

"This one's foaming at the mouth!" shouted the smaller man as he lifted the old dog down from the cart. The dog's body shook and then went still. "We'll never sell this dog. No one'll buy it." The big man came over to have a look.

"If it can still walk, just let it go." He said, shaking his head in annoyance. The smaller man opened the cage, tipping the dog out of it. The old dog managed to stand and it slowly hobbled away.

"Let's lock the other dogs up and go. We'll decide what to do with them tomorrow."

Kane was the last dog to be taken into the building. He hated being trapped in a cage where he had no room to move about.

The man carrying him threw the cage against the wall of the building, hurting Kane. He then closed the door of the building and slid a wooden plank across the door to keep the animals locked inside.

When the door closed the room went very dark.

There were other dogs in the building. Some barked, some howled.

Kane shivered. He was cold and frightened. He was locked in a cage, inside a locked building. Even if he could escape, which didn't seem possible, he had no idea where in London he had been taken to in the cart.

He thought about Adam.

Was he ever going to see him again or was this the end?

Chapter 5

Adam and Joseph walked for a long time around Barnes, asking everyone they met if they had seen a horse and cart that carried cages with dogs in. No one had.

"It's almost dark," said Joseph, "we need to look again in the morning when it's daylight."

"I suppose you're right," Adam's shoulders slumped.

"Come an' stay at ours. Ma and Pa won't mind. It will save you having to go back to Bucking'am Palace tonight and having to return in the morning," said Joseph. Adam realised he had nowhere else to stay.

"Thanks, that's kind. I will do if you don't mind."

They walked back the way they came, until they reached Limes Field where the football pitch was. Adam ran over to the two football posts. He wanted to see if the white painted line was there or would appear if he went near the posts.

There was only grass and mud though. No painted white line. He had no idea how to get the white line to appear. Even if he could make it appear, he had no intention of leaving Kane here all alone in 1863 though.

The boys crossed Limes Fields and kept walking, eventually arriving at a small run-down house.

"This is where our room is," said Joseph

"Only one room?" said Adam,

surprised. "You and your parents live in just one room?"

"Yes, with my three sisters as well."

"Six of you in one room?" Adam was beginning to realise what living in 1863 was like. "There won't be space for me as well though, will there?"

"Course there will. There's a gap on the floor next to me. We've got one spare blanket so you can use that to sleep on."

"On the floor," muttered Adam to himself.

"Yeah, just watch out for the rats though."

Adam was now very worried. As they opened the door the room was quite dark, apart from a few candles dotted around and the log fire in the corner. In the dim light Adam could make out all of Joseph's family.

"Ma, Pa, can my friend Adam stay

the night?" Joseph spoke very softly. He took his cap off his head and held it in his hands. "He's got nowhere to stay."

Joseph's father stood up from the wooden chair in the corner and studied Adam.

"Where are you from, sonny?"

"I live not far from Buckingham Palace, sir."

"You've got a bit lost then."

"Yes, sir," Adam looked around the room and saw a Christmas tree. "I like your tree." He thought it best to change the subject away from where he had come from.

"I put these decorations on," said his new friend, Joseph, proudly pointing at some walnuts wrapped in ribbons.

"And I did those," said one of Joseph's sisters, who walked over to the tree and pointed at some orange peel that spiralled down from some of the thin branches.

"I did the pine cones and cinnamon sticks," said another sister excitedly.

Over the next few hours they all chatted and Adam told the family what had happened to Kane and how they would continue their search for him the following day when there was daylight.

"Well, I don't think you'll find your dog, sonny," said Joseph's father, "but I don't see a problem with young Joseph helping you look tomorrow."

Before long it was bedtime and Adam was tired. He put the blanket he had been given, down on the floor, next to Joseph and used his rucksack as a pillow. He was glad he had his thick coat with him and he decided to leave his Wellington boots on as well. The candles were blown out by Joseph's father and darkness surrounded them all. One by one, Joseph and his sisters drifted off into sleep.

Adam was wide awake though. He wondered whether he would ever see Kane again. He also worried that if he couldn't find Kane, he might not be able to travel back to his own time.

He might be stranded in 1863 forever.

He suddenly realised that it might not just be Kane he wouldn't ever see again.

It might also be his mum and dad too.

Chapter 6

The following day was Friday and Adam and his new friend rose early to continue their search for Kane.

The boys looked all day long but couldn't find Adam's canine companion. They had searched for miles and miles and now both boys had sore feet from all the walking.

Eventually it fell dark again. The boys were tired and hungry.

"Come back to ours again, Adam," insisted Joseph.

"Can I?" Adam thought about the cold floor in his new friend's house but knew it was better than sleeping in the street. "If that's okay, I'd be very grateful."

Joseph's mother had some food for them when they arrived back.

"Boys, you eat some of this bread I've made. There's water in the jug too. The rest of us have already eaten."

"Thank you," both boys said, their stomachs rumbling. Joseph's family were so poor, this was all the food they had. Adam missed his favourite food and drink. Milk chocolate wouldn't be invented for another twelve years and Coca Cola, not for another twenty nine years! They didn't even exist in 1863.

Joseph was hungry though so he gobbled the crust of bread down but it barely filled his stomach. He washed it down with some brown coloured water which didn't taste very nice. It was better than nothing though.

That evening they all gathered around the log fire for warmth. It was only seven days until Christmas day and the children were all excited. "Last year I got an orange and a new penny for Christmas!" said one of the girls excitedly. "What did you get Adam?"

"A games console," he blurted out.

"What's that?" said another sister. Adam had momentarily forgotten that in 1863 they didn't even have televisions, never mind computer consoles.

"It's…um…a toy," replied Adam. He tried to get off the subject. "Do you sing Christmas carols?"

"Why, of course," said Joseph's mother, "what an excellent idea. How about singing Silent Night everyone?"

"Great idea, Ma," said Joseph and soon they were all gathered around the crackling fire, singing.

"Silent night,
holy night,
all is calm,
all is bright…"

For an hour Adam forgot all about his worries as they sang lots of carols and songs, including some Adam taught the family. They were songs that hadn't been invented yet.

Adam was enjoying being among such a wonderful family at Christmas. They had no money, few possessions and little food but they were happy.

After the carols had finished, Joseph walked over to the Christmas tree. He took down one of his own decorations from the tree, one he had spent time making. He walked back over to Adam.

"I want you to have this," Joseph said to his friend, holding out a walnut wrapped in a ribbon, in the palm of his hand, "for your Christmas tree back home." Adam was a little taken aback.

"Thank you," he said, "that's really kind. I'll keep it in here in one of the little pockets of my jacket so I don't lose it." He placed it in his pocket and smiled at Joseph.

"It's bedtime for you kids now as we've stayed up later than usual," said Joseph's mother. The children all obediently went over to where they slept and settled down for the night.

Adam struggled to sleep though. Joseph's dad saw their guest was still awake and knelt down next to him.

"Adam, I know you're Joseph's new friend but tomorrow it's time for you to make your way home." He put his hand on Adam's shoulder as he spoke to him. "You can stay tonight of course but I must insist that from tomorrow you find somewhere else to stay. I just can't afford to feed another child."

Adam gave a slow nod. The happiness of the evening had evaporated.

"I…understand."

"I'm sorry, sonny."

Adam curled up in his blanket on the floor and closed his eyes. He couldn't sleep, as he thought about his predicament.

He had no Kane,

No way to get back home,

And after tonight, he had nowhere to stay.

He was in trouble.

Chapter 7

It was Saturday and Kane had been trapped inside his wooden cage for two days. His legs and neck ached as he had not been allowed out.

Kane was a clever dog though and had come up with a plan. A plan of how to escape. He was worried whether it would work or not though.

He had seen how the men had let the old poorly dog go, when they thought he was of no use to them. So, for the last two days, every time one of the two men came into the building, Kane had pretended to be dead.

The door to the building had just opened again and Kane stayed as still as he could.

"This is the one I was talking about." said the smaller man to his companion. "He hasn't moved." The man kicked Kane's cage. Kane remained still.

"Leave it to me," said the bigger man. He grabbed the cage and slid out the wooden peg that held the lid closed. Kane was motionless. The giant man opened the lid. "Let's get you moving." He said and grabbed Kane's legs and dragged him out of the cage, onto the floor.

"What on earth!" he gasped. Kane suddenly sprung to life, jumped to his feet and dashed past his startled captor as fast as his stiff legs would carry him. The door to the building had been left open by the men. This was Kane's chance. He had to somehow try to get through it and away from them.

The smaller man though had seen what Kane was trying to do and now raced to shut the heavy door before Kane could escape.

Kane moved as fast as he could but just as he was about to get there the man reached the door and tried to shut it, to keep Kane trapped inside the building.

The big door had almost closed but there was a small gap left. Kane dived for it…

…and squeezed through!

The huge door slammed shut behind him, leaving the men inside.

Kane could hear the men shouting in anger at one another because one of their prized possessions had got out of their clutches. After a few seconds the men had opened the door again.

"Where is he?" They looked down the street, but Kane had gone. He was nowhere to be seen.

Kane had escaped.

Chapter 8

It was Saturday and the rest of Joseph's family had headed out early to the market.

"I just need to lock the door," said Joseph as he turned the key and then put it in the pocket of his tatty trousers. As soon as he did so, the metal key dropped through a hole in his trouser pocket and fell down his trouser leg and onto the floor.

"Good job that 'appened now," said a relieved Joseph as he scooped up the key. "I can't lose this or none of our family can get back in. This is the only key we 'ave."

"Here, pass it to me, I'll keep it in one of my coat pockets so it's safe."

"Thanks, Adam." Joseph handed him the key, which Adam pocketed. He zipped his pocket.

" 'ey what's that?" said Joseph. Adam looked at his coat.

"A zip."

"What's a zip?"

Adam smiled. He guessed that zips hadn't been invented yet, in 1863. In fact he had a vague recollection that they wouldn't be invented for another fifty years or so.

"It's a way of sealing the pocket, so your key won't fall out. It's an invention from where I come from."

Joseph reached over and tested pulling Adam's pocket zip up and down.

"What a great idea. Wish I 'ad one of those on my pockets."

"Come on Joseph, we need to find Kane. Let's make a start."

The boys continued their search for Kane for hours and hours, without finding him. As they walked along one of the cobbled streets not far from Limes Field they passed a large group of men.

"Where are all those men going?" said Joseph to Adam. "They're all wearing shorts."

"Of course! It's the first official football match today between Barnes and Richmond," exclaimed Adam.

"It must be starting soon then," said Joseph. "Let's follow them and watch the match for a bit."

The boys returned to Limes Field and watched the men getting ready to play. Ebenezer Cobb Morley was standing very nearby talking to his

Barnes players.

"The rules set out by the new English Football Association state that you are allowed to catch the ball but not carry it," said Morley, who had led the formation of the English Football Association, two months before. Morley continued to read to his players from the Football Association Minute Book, which explained the thirteen laws of football.

Adam overheard some of the rules and was a little surprised.

"The football players can catch the ball?" he whispered to Joseph.

"Yes of course. Any player can. They can't run with it or throw it though."

"Wow. Where I come from only the goalkeeper can catch the ball."

"What's a goalkeeper?" Joseph

frowned.

"It's a person who stays near their goal all the time," explained Adam, as he watched the men about to start the game. "Wow, I can't believe I'm getting to see the first official football match in history."

After a few minutes, the game started.

"This is funny," said Adam after the match had been under way for a while, "all thirty players just run after the person who's dribbling the ball. They all just dribble as well, rather than passing. They should pass more."

"Well, you can only pass backwards apparently, I overheard Ebenezer Morley saying that. That might be why they dribble, so they can go forward." Joseph was quite pleased with the bit of information he had managed to gather.

Whilst the boys were watching the football match, Kane the dog was walking through the streets of Barnes alone.

He was so relieved to have escaped from the horrible men but now was getting cold and lost.

He walked and walked for miles but didn't recognise any of the streets and couldn't find the football field.

He had no way of knowing where he was or where Adam was. Having not eaten or had any drink for two days, he was was feeling very weak as well.

After a long time of trotting through the streets he passed three young children, one of whom was kicking a misshapen brown football. Kane stopped and looked at the ball as they passed. The boys were talking quickly.

"Let's go and play a football match," said one of them.

Kane's ears pricked up when he heard the words, "football match." He couldn't understand what else they said but he had heard Adam say, "football match" many times. Kane suddenly got a huge boost. "They must be talking about the first ever football match that Adam had shown him sketches of in his football book," he thought. Kane stopped walking and turned his head round to watch the boys.

After the boys had walked on a little further, Kane changed direction and followed them. He made sure he was a long way behind so they wouldn't notice him.

Through the cobbled back

streets they weaved in between buildings. Kane continued to keep up with the boys at a distance.

After ten minutes, one of the boys kicked the ball high into the air and the trio sprinted after it onto the edge of a park. Kane's whole body slumped. He realised that it was their football match. Not the football match Kane needed to be at.

He trudged after the boys anyway.

The park was huge and Kane watched the boys play football for a little bit. He didn't have the enthusiasm to join in though. All his energy had gone and he just slumped down at the edge of the park.

Then a noise caught his attention. He could hear some shouting from the opposite side of the park. He strained his eyes to see what the commotion was.

There appeared to be a lot of men playing football in the distance.

Suddenly all of the cold, loneliness and worry vanished for a brief moment. Kane's ears pricked up and so did his tail.

"Could that be the match that Adam talked to him about?" he thought. "Could his master be there?"

He started running towards the match using his last reserves of energy, his four legs moving him as fast as they could. As he neared he looked at the spectators, desperate for one of them to be Adam.

He was getting closer and then spotted two boys watching and chatting.

One of them was Adam!

Kane barked and barked, as he ran faster than he ever had before.

"That sounds like....Kane!!" Adam turned to see his beloved dog charging towards him.

"It is Kane!!"

Kane reached his master and leapt into his arms. Adam hugged him tightly.

"You found us!" Adam looked at his dog, who was covered in mud but was so happy to see him.

For the next few minutes the boys made such a fuss of Kane. They could all watch the match together now.

Kane stood right next to his master. Adam looked down at him and could have sworn that his magical dog had a little smile on his face.

Chapter 9

"Not a great surprise that the score is 0-0, is it Kane?" Adam winked at Kane. He knew from reading his book that the match would finish goalless in a few minutes time. Joseph of course didn't know what the result would be.

"Pa says that Ebenezer Morley really wants his Barnes football team to be a success," said Joseph, as he watched Morley running after the ball. "If they win today, 'e thinks it'll give 'im a great chance of them making it as a football club, rather than being a rugby club."

Adam remembered what he had read in his book. Barnes drew 0-0 with Richmond and both end up as Rugby clubs. He decided not to say anything to Joseph.

"It's a shame we can't go on to the pitch and play," said Adam turning to Joseph, "just to say that we'd played in the first official match."

Kane's ears pricked up, he was sure that his master had just said they could go on and play.

All of a sudden Kane darted away from his master and ran onto the pitch. He started chasing after the ball, just as all the men were doing. Adam didn't notice until he had turned back around.

"Kane, no!" he shouted. Kane couldn't hear him though due to the shouting of the other spectators and players. Kane was quicker than the men. The player who had the ball at the time, kicked it out in front of him and chased after it but Kane had already got to it.

Kane dribbled it with his nose and headed towards the goal. The ground was very uneven though and the ball hit a divot in the ground and bounced away from Kane and ended up at the feet of a player who wasn't expecting it.

The player stopped the ball, looked at the goal in front of him and then toe-punted it past an opponent who was now standing near the goal. It hit one of the posts and went in! The goalscorer turned but didn't celebrate wildly. He just shook hands with a couple of his team mates.

"That doesn't count," shouted one of the opposition. He pointed at

Kane. "That dog got involved. Your player wouldn't have got the ball if it wasn't for that dog."

"Nonsense," shouted the goalscorer, "it's a goal."

A huge argument erupted between the players.

By this time Adam had run onto the pitch to try to pull Kane away from the trouble. He was worried for Kane's safety. As Adam reached Kane though he noticed something.

"Kane! Look at the goal." Adam had knelt beside his dog and pointed at the two goal posts.

There was a painted white line reflecting brightly in the afternoon sun, on the ground between the posts.

Adam and Kane immediately ignored the arguments going on behind them.

They looked at one another. Adam then turned round to Joseph and waved at him. There was no time to say goodbye.

The white painted line was starting to fade.

Adam and Kane were ten metres away from it.

"This is our chance, Kane! The time portal's open. If we run into the goal we might return back home!"

Adam didn't hesitate. He sprinted the ten metres as fast as he could. Kane was in hot pursuit a couple of metres behind.

The footballer's shouts faded behind them and at the instant that Adam crossed the white painted line, it all went very quiet.

Chapter 10

Adam and Kane came skidding out between the goalposts. A huge snow-covered field stretched out before them.

"My goodness. We're back, Kane!" Kane barked and wagged his tail. Adam looked behind him at the goal. The white painted line was fading away. There was now no 1863 football match, no players, no muddy field. They had returned to the present day. "What a relief," said Adam, blowing air from his cheeks, "we're home."

"Joseph will have wondered where

we vanished to." Adam reflected, his smile disappearing as he thought about his friend. "I wish we could've said goodbye to him."

He looked all around. "Hey, there's my football. I didn't have time to get it when we travelled back in time. No one's taken it."

An elderly couple were walking towards them on the snow covered path nearby.

"Hi there," said Adam to the couple, "I just wondered…what's the date today?"

"It's 17th December," the husband answered, "only eight days to Christmas day, young man."

"Thank you," Adam smiled, "Merry Christmas!"

"Merry Christmas to you too," the wife replied, as the old couple continued on their walk.

Adam frowned as he tried to work out what had happened. He crouched down next to Kane and stroked him.

"This is odd, Kane. It was Thursday 17th December at the start of this adventure, when you came bounding onto my bed and woke me up, because I remember seeing it on my clock. Then we travelled back in time to 1863 and spent two days there." Kane cocked his head to the side as he listened intently. "Yet we've arrived back in our time on the 17th December, which is the same day we left." Adam scratched his chin. "It's just as though no time had passed at all here." He looked at his football and then the ground. "There are no other footprints around and no one's taken my football. I think we might have returned to our time just a few moments after we left it."

"Come on boy, let's get back home, I'm starving. We need to get you some food and water as well. Time might not have gone by here but you and I have lived an extra couple of days and haven't had much to eat!"

Kane barked in agreement as Adam scooped his football up. He felt on his back for his rucksack, to put his ball into. There was nothing on his back though.

"Oh no, I've left my rucksack!" Adam thought back to where he last had it, "When I ran on to the pitch to get you, Kane, I left it with Joseph. It's back in 1863." Adam groaned. "It had my favourite football book in it as well." He sighed. "Gutting."

"Well, at least we got back safely. That's the main thing," Kane barked. "I'm so annoyed I've lost my book though." Adam started walking, with Kane trotting beside him.

"What an adventure that was. I can't believe we got to see the first official football match in history and you even got involved in it, Kane." Adam laughed as a snow flake drifted to the ground in front of him. He looked up to the white sky. "Hey, it's snowing." He reached out his hand and a snowflake landed on it. "It's so good to be back."

Adam patted Kane as he skipped along. He started singing as the snow fell all around them…

"Sleigh bells ring, are you listening

In the lane, snow is glistening

A beautiful sight, we're happy tonight

Walking in a winter wonderland…"

After a walk where Adam threw a

few snow balls back at some younger kids who wanted to play, the pair rounded the corner of their cul-de-sac to see their home in front of them.

Adam reached the porch, stamped his boots on the step outside the house, knocking the snow off them and then opened the front door.

"Wow, how warm is that, Kane?" They were hit by the heat from inside the house. Adam took his gloves off and put them on the table by the door and then removed his boots.

"Never thought I would be so glad to feel a radiator again. All that time without heating was a nightmare."

"Dad, Mum, we're home!" he shouted.

"Did you have a good time?" came the voice of his mother from upstairs, who knew nothing about the adventure they had been on. She just thought they had been out playing for the day.

"Sort of!" Adam shouted as he skidded into the kitchen, opened the fridge and started eating everything he could see.

"There you go boy," he said, filling Kane's bowl to the brim with dogfood. Kane wolfed it down.

After filling their stomachs, Adam and Kane went into the lounge and Adam threw some more logs on the fire. He and Kane sat in front of it, feeling the warmth from the orange flames before them.

"Your football team, Barnes, did well last night I see, Adam," said his dad, walking into the lounge, "ten points clear at the top of the Premier League now."

"What do you mean 'my football team Barnes'?" said Adam, very puzzled. "There's no such Premier League team as Barnes." Adam looked at his dad as though he was mad.

"Of course there is," his dad laughed, "you've supported them for years." He showed the newspaper to Adam. "Here you go."

"I don't support Barnes. You know perfectly well that I support Newcastle, Dad." Adam took the newspaper and looked at the league table. Sure enough it showed a team called, Barnes FC at the top of the Premier League. They were positioned one place above Newcastle!

"I don't understand it." Adam looked at his dad, very confused. "Barnes FC weren't in the Premier

League. I didn't think they existed. Why would you say I support them?"

"You've supported them ever since you were little," replied Adam's father with a chuckle. "The day I told you that Barnes had played Richmond in the first official match in history and that a dog had helped score the winning goal, you decided to support them. You liked them even more when you found out they went on the longest winning streak in history after that first match."

"Barnes didn't win the first match though, it was 0-0 against Richmond," said Adam indignantly.

"No, it was 1-0. Look at this, there's an article in the newspaper, here." Adam took the paper and started reading the article. Sure enough, it explained that the score of the very first match in history was

Barnes 1-0 Richmond. Adam looked at Kane.

"Something's wrong, Kane," he whispered. He was still annoyed that his dad thought he supported Barnes FC which was a team that he was sure didn't exist.

What was going on?

Adam suddenly had a thought on how to prove who he supported. "My room's covered in Newcastle posters! That'll prove who I support and it certainly isn't Barnes FC!" Adam said to his dad.

Before his dad could reply, Adam darted out of the room into the hall. He skipped up the stairs, with the newspaper in his hand, passed the small Christmas tree with twinkling lights on the landing and opened the door to his room. He stood and stared at the walls. His eyes got wider.

"What on earth!" Adam exclaimed as he scanned all the posters. "These posters all say Barnes FC on them. Where are all my Newcastle posters?"

Adam slumped down onto the side of his bed.

"What's happened, Kane?" Adam said, as his canine friend bounded into the room after him. Adam stayed very still as he thought it all through.

"Wait a minute…" He clicked his fingers as he realised something. "Dad said that Barnes FC won the very first match 1-0 and that a dog went onto the pitch and set up the winning goal." Adam looked at the newspaper article again and started reading it. "It says here that the dog was a black labrador…" Adam stopped talking and looked down at his dog. His eyes widened. Kane was a black labrador.

"Kane. This dog they're writing about in the newspaper article...could it be you?" Adam blew out a deep breath.

"My goodness Kane, the score in 1863 should have been 0-0 but because you ran on the pitch and passed the ball to that man, he scored a goal, which he wouldn't have done without you passing it to him. So you helped change the score from 0-0 to 1-0!" Kane whined. "This meant Barnes went on to win and that inspired them to keep on winning."

Adam continued reading the newspaper article aloud to Kane. "Due to their incredible success at football, Barnes stayed as a football club, didn't play rugby anymore and became the most successful football club in history." Kane barked in surprise.

"Can you believe it Kane? One little action you did in 1863 caused the whole of football history to change!" Adam shook his head. "This is incredible." Adam then pondered the situation. "It's not right though. For a start, Newcastle United aren't top! I don't see how we can change it though… without travelling back in time to 1863."

At that point Adam put his hand in his coat pocket. He felt something cold and solid.

"What's this?" he said as he pulled a metal object from his jacket pocket. "A key." He suddenly realised where the key was from.

"Oh no!" he gasped, "This is Joseph's key. It's the only key his family have got and Joseph gave it to me to look after! Joseph and his family won't be able to get into their house. They will end up out in the cold, sleeping in the streets!"

Adam looked at Kane who had a worried expression on his face. Adam knew they had to sort all of this mess out. There was only one option.

"We have to travel back in time to 1863, Kane."

Chapter 11

"Kane and I are going out to play again mum!" Adam shouted as he took the stairs, two at a time. In the hallway by the front door he pulled his boots on and stuffed his gloves in his pockets.

"Well, don't be too long, it'll be dark soon. The nights draw in early remember," shouted his mum, "and can you take that bag of stuff that's at the front door, and drop it off at the charity shop, please."

"Sure, mum. See you later!" Adam grabbed the plastic bag and slammed the front door shut behind them, after Kane had jumped out into the snow.

After a good walk, the pair reached the park and could see the two goalposts in the distance.

They stopped running and now walked towards the only grassy area, where the trees sheltered the two mysterious goal posts.

"The white goal line!" Adam said as he looked at a bright line stretching from one goalpost to the other. "It's there!" Adam paused for a moment and looked at Kane. "It's reappeared." He took a deep breath. "Do we do it Kane? Do we try to get back to 1863?"

He turned Joseph's key around in his hand. "We can't leave Joseph and his family out in the cold. Plus we need to sort that football match result out somehow." Kane barked.

"Good point, Kane. I need my rucksack and book too."

Adam moved forward. He was a few feet away from the line. He took a deep breath and gave a big nod of his head.

"Let's do this." He walked the remaining few steps and crossed the line between the posts, with his canine companion following a few paces behind.

Suddenly the snow in the park vanished and was replaced by the muddy football field. They had travelled back in time again.

It was 1863.

At the instant Adam stepped into 1863, he was sure he saw the back of Kane disappearing past him going in the opposite direction through the goal. A second later though Kane appeared behind him.

"Very strange," thought Adam. He didn't have long to think about it though because in front of him stood the same group of footballers. He watched as the Barnes goalscorer was shaking hands with other Barnes players.

"Kane, they've just scored the goal to make it 1-0. We've returned at the exact instant that we left. I think I might even have just seen you leaving!" Kane cocked his head at Adam. "To these players, it will seem as though we've never departed."

"You boy! And that confounded dog of yours! You've got some explaining to do!" The Richmond players were walking towards Adam and they looked very angry.

Adam, who was a very quick thinker, suddenly remembered something that he had read in his football book about Ebenezer Morley's football rule book. He wondered if he could turn Morley's rules to his advantage and get the goal ruled out. Looking at the men striding towards him he decided this was his only option.

"Where's Ebenezer Morley?" Adam shouted. He was surprised by how authoritative his own voice sounded. It was time to give his plan a try. "That was not a goal!" Adam stated.

The men stopped, a little surprised. The player nearest Adam, turned and pointed Morley out.

"He's over there."

"Mr Morley!" shouted Adam. "The Richmond players demand to see the

'Football Association Minute book!" Adam had remembered the name of it just in time. He was also sure he could recall some of the rules he had read in his favourite book when he and Kane were in the igloo.

"Why is this lad wanting to see Morley?" One of the Richmond players said to another.

"Not sure," his team mate replied, "I'm interested to know though."

The Richmond players watched as Adam strode boldly over to where Ebenezer Morley was plucking his rulebook from his bag at the side of the pitch. Morley's glee at his team's goal was now wavering.

Joseph, who had remained on the sidelines during the commotion, was wandering over as well, with Adam's rucksack in his hand. Adam smiled at him and Joseph gave him a grin.

"Well, what do they want with the rule book, boy?" said Morley aggressively.

"They want me to have a look at it, sir." Morley frowned. Adam wasn't sure whether the organiser was going to hand it over. "They can't read." Adam explained. Adam guessed that quite a lot of people couldn't read in the olden days, so it was hopefully a good enough reason to persuade Morley to hand the book over to him. "I can read very well though." Adam could see Morley thinking this last comment over in his mind.

"Very well. If you must."

He handed the book over and Adam flicked through to one of the rules that he was looking for.

"Here it is," said Adam triumphantly, "rule 11 states that a player shall not throw the ball or pass it to another." Adam looked at Ebenezer Morley. "My dog passed it."

"Nonsense, you're not allowed to pass the ball if you catch it. You can pass the ball if it's on the ground." replied Morley, getting annoyed. Now Adam was beginning to panic a little. That was the only argument he could think of and he had misinterpreted it. Morley had just dismissed it.

Adam had a quick scan through the pages.

"Ah ha! The rules throughout the book, refer to 'players'," said Adam, as he realised he had a better argument. "My dog wasn't one of the 'players', therefore his touch can't have been allowed." Morley looked furiously at Adam, grabbed his rulebook off the boy and threw it back into his bag. He stared at Adam for a couple of seconds and then shook his head in disappointment. The boy was right.

"The goal does not stand!" Morley shouted to all the players. He was very annoyed. "The score is still 0-0." He bellowed.

His own Barnes teammates let out a collective moan, whilst a few of the Richmond players slapped each other on the back. Ebenezer Morley ran back onto the pitch to get the game started again.

"That was funny!" Joseph said. He had now reached Adam and Kane and handed the rucksack back to its rightful owner. "It's almost as though you'd seen those brand new rules before?"

"I was just lucky." Adam said, smiling, as he slung his rucksack over his shoulder. "I guessed there might have been something I could use, I just scanned the pages quickly." Adam certainly couldn't explain to Joseph that he had read about the rules in a book from the future, nor his reasons for wanting to cancel out the goal. Joseph wouldn't have understood.

They watched the last few minutes of the match together, with Kane under strict instructions not to go onto the pitch. Eventually the 15-a-side match came to an end. It was full-time and the score was 0-0.

"It's time for us to go back home, Joseph. Thank you so much for everything, especially helping search for Kane and letting me stay at your home."

"My pleasure," replied the urchin boy. Kane barked at Adam.

"Oh goodness, yes, I almost forgot." Adam tapped his head. He reached into his pocket. "Here's your key, Joseph. Take care of it. Don't put it in that pocket of yours with the hole in it though."

"Thanks, I won't," laughed Joseph. "They've all got 'oles in 'em. I'll just hold it. Pa would be furious if I lost it."

Adam realised he still had the charity bag hanging from his wrist, that his mum had told him to take. "I've got something else for you too." Out of the bag, Adam pulled one of his old coats and a pair of shoes he had outgrown. "I reckon these will be about the right size for you."

"For me?" Joseph's eyes lit up. "I've never 'ad shoes!" He gazed at the worn plain black trainers with awe. He then looked at the coat.

"It's got those things that go up and down!"

"Zips," said Adam laughing. "Here, put it on."

"I can't believe it," Joseph put the coat on and fumbled with the zip, eventually getting it to zip up. He tried his new shoes on, fascinated by the velcro fasteners. He kept on lifting them off and putting them down again.

"I can't believe it. I've never had shoes before."

"So you said," Adam chuckled.

"Are you sure I can have these?"

"Of course, they're my gift to you." Adam looked over at the goalposts and then back at Joseph who was trying out all his zips. "Joseph, it's time for Kane and I to go home." Joseph's face dropped and his shoulders slumped.

"Yes, I know." He gave the pair a reluctant smile. "Goodbye, Adam. Bye, Kane." Joseph stroked the dog. "Don't you go running off again!" Kane barked.

"Bye, Joseph," replied Adam.

Both dog and master headed towards the two goal posts they had come through, whilst Joseph set off in the opposite direction.

As Adam and Kane approached the posts, a white painted line appeared before their eyes.

Adam looked behind him. All the players were chatting to each other at the opposite side of the pitch and Joseph was concentrating on his zips as he wandered home. If they left now, no one would see them vanish into thin air.

"Right Kane, lets hope this takes us back home."

The pair stepped over the white line.

Chapter 12

Adam and Kane re-appeared back in their own time and started walking home. It was mid afternoon now and starting to get dark. The moon was out and the snow was falling. Brightly coloured lights hung between the trees which lined the roadside at the edge of the park. It seemed like a winter wonderland to them both.

"Come on, Kane, let's take a different route home. I want to have a quick look through the window of the toy shop."

The streets were packed with

people slushing through the snow as they did their Christmas shopping. A brass band was playing at the far end of the road and the sound of Christmas carols floated through the air. They reached the quaint little toy shop.

"There it is, Kane," said Adam as he peered at a computer game through the window of the store. The door jangled as some customers walked past them and into the shop. Adam's breath steamed up the square window pane as he looked through it. "I really hope I get that new football game for Christmas." After a moment though he remembered what they needed to do.

"Come on, we have to get back. There's something important we need to check." Kane barked in agreement.

"Mum, Dad, we're home!" shouted Adam as he kicked off his wellies and removed his gloves. Kane shook all the snow off his fur as he came through the door.

"We're in the lounge," shouted Adam's dad.

Adam smiled as he and Kane entered the room. The fire was roaring and Adam's mum was hanging some glittery baubles she had just bought, onto their Christmas tree. The empty red and white Christmas stockings were fixed to the mantlepiece and some presents, no doubt for relatives, were spread out under the tree.

"Here, mum." Adam unzipped one of the pockets in his coat. "This is a decoration they used to have in the days when Queen Victoria was alive." His mum looked a little surprised. "It's a walnut wrapped in a ribbon. They used to hang orange peel on their trees as well for decoration," explained Adam.

"I never knew that," said his mum, looking a little impressed at being taught something new. Adam then turned to his dad.

"Do you know how Barnes Football Club did last weekend, dad?" His father looked up from his paper.

"Who?" he replied, "Never heard of them." Adam grinned. He looked at Kane.

"That's encouraging," he whispered to his dog, "now to find out for sure."

Adam charged out of the lounge, ran up the stairs and into his bedroom.

Which posters was he going to see?

Would they still be Barnes FC posters or had time been altered back to normal and they would be his own Newcastle United posters?

"The posters, Kane! They're my Newcastle posters, not those Barnes FC ones!" Kane jumped up and down with excitement as Adam spoke. "We went back in time to 1863, kept the match score as Barnes 0-0 Richmond and so Barnes didn't win, so they didn't go on a huge winning streak. They didn't become the best team ever. History is restored!" He sat on his bed, patted Kane and reflected on the situation.

"Joseph got his key back and so he can get into his house and we rescued my rucksack and book. Plus Newcastle are back on top of the league where they should be!" He gave Kane a big hug.

"Not only did we get to see the first ever official football match but you even played in it and everything has ended okay!" Adam looked at his magical dog, his face beaming.

"We did it, Kane. It was a close one but we did it."

Factual History

Ebenezer Cobb Morley

Ebenezer Cobb Morley (1831 – 1924) was a Solicitor and English sportsman and is regarded as the father of the Football Association (FA) and modern football.

Morley was born in Hull, moving to Barnes in 1858 forming the Barnes Club, a founding member of the FA, in 1862.

Morley was the FA's first secretary (1863–1866) and its second president (1867–1874) and drafted the first Laws of the Game at his home in Barnes.

As a player, he played in the first ever match, against Richmond in 1863. He was described as 'a most effective dribbler'.

The FA and the first official match

Morley wrote to Bell's Life, a popular newspaper, suggesting that football should have a set of rules, in the same way that the MCC had for cricket. His letter led to the first historic meeting at the Freemasons' Tavern in London. The FA was formed there on 26 October 1863. It was the world's first official football body and for this reason is not preceded with the word English.

'Football', they thought, would be a blend of handling and dribbling. Players would be able to handle the ball: a fair catch accompanied by 'a mark with the heel' would win a free kick. The sticking point was 'hacking', or kicking an opponent on the leg.

The laws originally drafted by Morley were finally approved at the sixth meeting, on 8 December 1863, and there would be no hacking.

An inaugural game using the new FA rules was initially scheduled for Battersea Park on 2 January 1864, but enthusiastic members of the FA could not wait for the new year and an experimental game was played at Limes Field on 19 December 1863 between Morley's Barnes team and their neighbours Richmond. The final score was 0-0.

Sources:
The Official History of the Football Association (1991)
theFA.com (http://www.thefa.com/about-football-association/what-we-do/history)
Wikipedia (https://en.wikipedia.org/wiki/The_Football_Association)
Wikipedia (https://en.wikipedia.org/wiki/Ebenezer_Cobb_Morley)

The 13 laws of the game in 1863

1. The maximum length of the ground shall be 200 yards, the maximum breadth shall be 100 yards, the length and breadth shall be marked off with flags; and the goals shall be defined by two upright posts, 8 yards apart, without any tape or bar across them

2. The winner of the toss shall have the choice of goals. The game shall be commenced by a place kick from the centre of the ground by the side losing the toss, the other side shall not approach within 10 yards of the ball until it is kicked off

3. After a goal is won the losing side shall kick off and goals shall be changed

4. A goal shall be won when the ball passes between the goal posts or over the space between the goal posts (at whatever height), not being thrown, knocked on, or carried

5. When the ball is in touch the first player who touches it shall throw it from the point on the boundary line where it left the ground, in a direction at right angles with the boundary line and it shall not be in play until it has touched the ground

6. When a player has kicked the ball any one of the same side who is nearer to the opponent's goal line is out of play and may not touch the ball himself nor in any way whatever prevent any other player from doing so until the ball has been played; but no player is out of play when the ball is kicked from behind the goal line

7. In case the ball goes behind the goal line, if a player on the

side to whom the goal belongs first touches the ball, one of his side shall be entitled to a free kick from the goal line at the point opposite the place where the ball shall be touched. If a player of the opposite side first touches the ball, one of his side shall be entitled to a free kick (but at the goal only) from a point 15 yards from the goal line opposite the place where the ball is touched. The opposing side shall stand behind their goal line until he has had his kick

8. If a player makes a fair catch he shall be entitled to a free kick, provided he claims it by making a mark with his heel at once; ad in order to take such kick he may go as far back as he pleases, and no player on the opposite side shall advance beyond his mark until he has kicked

9. No player shall carry the ball

10. Neither tripping nor hacking shall be allowed and no player shall use his hands to hold or push his adversary

11. A player shall not throw the ball or pass it to another

12. No player shall take the ball from the ground with his hands while it is in play under any pretence whatever

13. No player shall wear projecting nails, iron plates, or gutta percha on the soles or heels of his boots

Books by Adrian Lobley

Kane series (Historical Fiction) (Ages 7-10)

The Football Maths Book series (Maths)(Ages 4-10)

A Learn to Read Book series (Reading) (Ages 4-5)

The Ridiculous Adventures of Sidebottom and McPlop (Humour) (Ages 7-10)

For more information visit: www.adrianlobley.com